CARLOS FUENTES

AURA

ANDRE DEUTSCH

This edition first published 1990
by André Deutsch Limited
105–106 Great Russell Street, London WC1B 3LJ

ISBN 0 233 98470 4 hardback
ISBN 0 233 98562 X paperback

Typeset by AKM Associates (UK) Ltd
Ajmal House, Hayes Road, Southall, London
Printed and bound in Great Britain by
WBC Ltd, Bristol and Maesteg

Man hunts and struggles.
Woman intrigues and dreams;
she is the mother of fantasy,
the mother of the gods.
She has second sight,
the wings that enable her to fly
to the infinite of
desire and the imagination . . .
The gods are like men:
they are born and they die
on a woman's breast . . .

JULES MICHELET

AᴜʀA

1

You're reading the advertisement: an offer like this isn't made every day. You read it and reread it. It seems to be addressed to you and nobody else. You don't even notice when the ash from your cigarette falls into the cup of tea you ordered in this cheap, dirty café. You read it again. "Wanted, young historian, conscientious, neat. Perfect knowledge colloquial French." Youth... knowledge of French, preferably after living in France for a while . . . "Four thousand pesos a month, all meals, comfortable bedroom-study." All that's missing is your name. The advertisement should have two more words, in bigger, blacker type: Felipe Montero. Wanted, Felipe Montero, formerly on scholarship at the Sorbonne, historian full of useless facts, accustomed to digging among yellowed documents, part-time teacher in private schools, nine hundred pesos a month. But if you read that, you'd be suspicious, and take it as a joke. "Address, Donceles *815*." No telephone. Come in person.

You leave a tip, reach for your brief case, get up. You wonder if another young historian, in the same situation you are, has seen the same advertisement, has got ahead of you and taken the job already. You walk down to the corner, trying to forget this idea. As you wait for the bus, you run over the dates you must have on the tip of your tongue so that your sleepy pupils will respect you. The bus is coming now, and you're staring at the tips of your black shoes. You've got to be prepared. You put your hand in your pocket, search among the coins, and finally take out thirty centavos. You've got to be prepared. You grab the handrail—the bus slows down but doesn't stop—and jump aboard. Then you shove your way forward, pay the driver the thirty centavos, squeeze yourself in among the passengers already standing in the aisle, hang onto the over-head rail, press your brief case tighter under your left arm, and automatically put your left hand over the back pocket where you keep your wallet.

This day is just like any other day, and you don't remember the advertisement until the next morning, when you sit down in the same café and order breakfast and open your newspaper. You come to the advertising section and there it is again: *young historian*. The job is still open. You reread the advertisement, lingering over the final words: four thousand pesos.

It's surprising to know that anyone lives on Donceles Street. You always thought that nobody lived in the old centre of the city. You walk slowly,

trying to pick out the number *815* in that con-
glomeration of old colonial mansions, all of them
converted into repair shops, jewelry shops, shoe
stores, drugstores. The numbers have been changed,
painted over, confused. A *13* next to a *200*. An old
plaque reading *47* above a scrawl in blurred char-
coal: *Now 924.* You look up at the second stories. Up
there, everything is the same as it was. The jukeboxes
don't disturb them. The mercury streetlights don't
shine in. The cheap merchandise on sale along the
street doesn't have any effect on that upper level; on
the baroque harmony of the carved stones; on the
battered stone saints with pigeons clustering on their
shoulders; on the latticed balconies, the copper
gutters, the sandstone gargoyles; on the greenish
curtains that darken the long windows; on that
window from which someone draws back when you
look at it. You gaze at the fanciful vines carved over
the doorway, then lower your eyes to the peeling
wall and discover *815, formerly 69.*

You rap vainly with the knocker, that copper head
of a dog, so worn and smooth that it resembles the
head of a canine foetus in a museum of natural
science. It seems as if the dog is grinning at you and
you let go of the cold metal. The door opens at the
first light push of your fingers, but before going in
you give a last look over your shoulder, frowning at
the long line of stalled cars that growl, honk, and
belch out the unhealthy fumes of their impatience.
You try to retain some single image of that in-
different outside world.

You close the door behind you and peer into the

darkness of a roofed alleyway. It must be a patio of some sort, because you can smell the mould, the dampness of the plants, the rotting roots, the thick drowsy aroma. There isn't any light to guide you, and you're searching in your coat pocket for the box of matches when a sharp, thin voice tells you, from a distance: "No, it isn't necessary. Please. Walk thirteen steps forward and you'll come to a stairway at your right. Come up, please. There are twenty-two steps. Count them."

Thirteen. To the right. Twenty-two.

The dank smell of the plants is all around you as you count out your steps, first on the paving-stones, then on the creaking wood, spongy from the damp-ness. You count to twenty-two in a low voice and then stop, with the matchbox in your hand, and the brief case under your arm. You knock on a door that smells of old pine. There isn't any knocker. Finally you push it open. Now you can feel a carpet under your feet, a thin carpet, badly laid. It makes you trip and almost fall. Then you notice the greyish filtered light that reveals some of the humps.

"Señora," you say, because you seem to re-member a woman's voice. "Señora . . ."

"Now turn to the left. The first door. Please be so kind."

You push the door open: you don't expect any of them to be latched, you know they all open at a push. The scattered lights are braided in your eyelashes, as if you were seeing them through a silken net. All you can make out are the dozens of flickering lights. At last you can see that they're votive lights, all set on

brackets or hung between unevenly-spaced panels.
They cast a faint glow on the silver objects, the
crystal flasks, the gilt-framed mirrors. Then you see
the bed in the shadows beyond, and the feeble
movement of a hand that seems to be beckoning to
you.

But you can't see her face until you turn your back
on that galaxy of religious lights. You stumble to the
foot of the bed, and have to go around it in order to
get to the head of it. A tiny figure is almost lost in its
immensity. When you reach out your hand, you
don't touch another hand, you touch the ears and
thick fur of a creature that's chewing silently and
steadily, looking up at you with its glowing red eyes.
You smile and stroke the rabbit that's crouched
beside her hand. Finally you shake hands, and her
cold fingers remain for a long while in your sweating
palm.

"I'm Felipe Montero. I read your advertisement."

"Yes, I know. I'm sorry, there aren't any chairs."

"That's all right. Don't worry about it."

"Good. Please let me see your profile. No, I can't
see it well enough. Turn toward the light. That's
right. Excellent."

"I read your advertisement . . ."

"Yes, of course. Do you think you're qualified?
Avez-vous fait des études?"

"*A Paris, madame.*"

"*Ah, oui, ça me fait plaisir, toujours, toujours,
d'entendre . . . oui . . . vous savez . . . on était tellement
habitué . . . et après . . .*"

You move aside so that the light from the candles

and the reflections from the silver and crystal show you the silk coif that must cover a head of very white hair, and that frames a face so old it's almost childlike. Her whole body is covered by the sheets and the feather pillows and the high, tightly buttoned white collar, all except for her arms, which are wrapped in a shawl, and her pallid hands resting on her stomach. You can only stare at her face until a movement of the rabbit lets you glance furtively at the crusts and bits of bread scattered on the worn-out red silk of the pillows.

"I'll come directly to the point, I don't have many years ahead of me, Señor Montero, and therefore I decided to break a lifelong rule and place an advertisement in the newspaper."

"Yes, that's why I'm here."

"Of course. So you accept."

"Well, I'd like to know a little more."

"Yes. You're wondering."

She sees you glance at the night table, the different-coloured bottles, the glasses, the aluminium spoons, the row of pillboxes, the other glasses—all stained with whitish liquids—on the floor within reach of her hand. Then you notice that the bed is hardly raised above the level of the floor. Suddenly the rabbit jumps down and disappears in the shadows.

"I can offer you four thousand pesos."

"Yes, that's what the advertisement said today."

"Ah, then it came out."

"Yes, it came out."

"It has to do with the memoirs of my husband,

General Llorente. They must be put in order before I die. I want them to be published. I decided that a short time ago."

"But the General himself? Wouldn't he be able to . . ."

"He died sixty years ago, Señor. They're his unfinished memoirs. They have to be completed before I die."

"But . . ."

"I can tell you everything. You'll learn to write in my husband's own style. You'll only have to arrange and read his manuscripts to become fascinated by his style . . . his clarity : . . his . . . "

"Yes, I understand."

"Saga, Saga. Where are you? *Ici*, Saga!"

"Who?"

"My companion."

"The rabbit?"

"Yes. She'll come back."

When you raise your eyes, which you've been keeping lowered, her lips are closed but you can hear her words again—"She'll come back"—as if the old lady were pronouncing them at that instant. Her lips remain still. You look in back of you and you're almost blinded by the gleam from the religious objects. When you look at her again you see that her eyes have opened very wide, and that they're clear, liquid, enormous, almost the same colour as the yellowish whites around them, so that only the black dots of the pupils mar that clarity. It's lost a moment later in the heavy folds of her lowered eyelids, as if she wanted to protect that glance which is now hiding at the back of its dry cave.

"Then you'll stay here. Your room is upstairs. It's sunny there."

"It might be better if I didn't trouble you, Señora. I can go on living where I am and work on the manuscripts there."

"My conditions are that you have to live here. There isn't much time left."

"I don't know if . . ."

"Aura . . ."

The old woman moves for the first time since you entered her room. As she reaches out her hand again, you sense that agitated breathing beside you, and another hand reaches out to touch the Señoras fingers. You look around and a girl is standing there, a girl whose whole body you can't see because she's standing so close to you and her arrival was so unexpected, without the slightest sound—not even those sounds that can't be heard but are real anyway because they're remembered immediately after-wards, because in spite of everything they're louder than the silence that accompanies them.

"I told you she'd come back."

"Who?"

"Aura. My companion. My niece."

"Good afternoon."

The girl nods and at the same instant the old lady imitates her gesture.

"This is Señor Montero. He's going to live with us."

You move a few steps so that the light from the candles won't blind you. The girl keeps her eyes closed, her hands at her sides. She doesn't look at you at first, then little by little she opens her eyes as if she were afraid of the light. Finally you can see that those eyes are sea green and that they surge, break to foam, grow calm again, then surge again like a wave. You look into them and tell yourself it isn't true, because they're beautiful green eyes just like all the beautiful green eyes you've ever known. But you can't deceive yourself: those eyes do surge, do change, as if offering you a landscape that only you can see and desire.

"Yes. I'm going to live with you."

2

The old woman laughs sharply and tells you that she is grateful for your kindness and that the girl will show you to your room. You're thinking about the salary of four thousand pesos, and how the work should be pleasant because you like these jobs of careful research that don't include physical effort or going from one place to another or meeting people you don't want to meet. You're thinking about this as you follow her out of the room, and you discover that you've got to follow her with your ears instead of your eyes: you follow the rustle of her skirt, the rustle of taffeta, and you're anxious now to look into her eyes again. You climb the stairs behind that sound in the darkness, and you're still unused to the obscurity. You remember it must be about six in the afternoon, and the flood of light surprises you when Aura opens the door to your bedroom—another door without a latch—and steps aside to tell you: "This is your room. We'll expect you for supper in an hour."

She moves away with the same faint rustle of taffeta, and you weren't able to see her face again.

You close the door and look up at the skylight that serves as a roof. You smile when you find that the evening light is blinding compared with the darkness in the rest of the house, and smile again when you try out the mattress on the gilded metal bed. Then you glance around the room: a red wool rug, olive and gold wallpaper, an easy chair covered in red velvet, an old walnut desk with a green leather top, an old Argand lamp with its soft glow for your nights of research, and a bookshelf over the desk in reach of your hand. You walk over to the other door, and on pushing it open you discover an outmoded bathroom: a four-legged bathtub with little flowers painted on the porcelain, a blue hand basin, an old-fashioned toilet. You look at yourself in the large oval mirror on the door of the wardrobe—it's also walnut—in the bathroom hallway. You move your heavy eyebrows and wide thick lips, and your breath fogs the mirror. You close your black eyes, and when you open them again the mirror has cleared. You stop holding your breath and run your hand through your dark, limp hair; you touch your fine profile, your lean cheeks; and when your breath hides your face again you're repeating her name: "Aura."

After smoking two cigarettes while lying on the bed, you get up, put on your jacket, and comb your hair. You push the door open and try to remember the route you followed coming up. You'd like to

19

leave the door open so that the lamplight could guide you, but that's impossible because the springs close it behind you. You could enjoy playing with that door, swinging it back and forth. You don't do it. You could take the lamp down with you. You don't do it. This house will always be in darkness, and you've got to learn it and relearn it by touch. You grope your way like a blind man, with your arms stretched out wide, feeling your way along the wall, and by accident you turn on the light-switch. You stop and blink in the bright middle of that long, empty hall. At the end of it you can see the bannister and the spiral staircase.

You count the stairs as you go down: another custom you're got to learn in Señora Llorente's house. You take a step backward when you see the reddish eyes of the rabbit, which turns its back on you and goes hopping away.

You don't have time to stop in the lower hall-way because Aura is waiting for you at a half-open stained-glass door, with a candelabra in her hand. You walk toward her, smiling, but you stop when you hear the painful yowling of a number of cats— yes, you stop to listen, next to Aura, to be sure that they're cats—and then follow her to the parlour.

"It's the cats," Aura tells you. "There are lots of rats in this part of the city."

You go through the parlour: furniture upholstered in faded silk; glass-fronted cabinets containing porcelain figurines, musical clocks, medals, glass balls; carpets with Persian patterns; pictures of rustic scenes; green velvet curtains. Aura is dressed in green.

"Is your room comfortable?"

"Yes. But I have to get my things from the place where . . ."

"It won't be necessary. The servant has already gone for them."

"You shouldn't have bothered."

You follow her into the dining room. She places the candelabra in the middle of the table. The room feels damp and cold. The four walls are panelled in dark wood carved in Gothic style, with fretwork arches and large rosettes. The cats have stopped yowling. When you sit down, you notice that four places have been set. There are two large, covered plates and an old, grimy bottle.

Aura lifts the cover from one of the plates. You breathe in the pungent odour of the liver and onions she serves you, then you pick up the old bottle and fill the cut-glass goblets with that thick red liquid. Out of curiosity you try to read the label on the wine bottle, but the grime has obscured it. Aura serves you some whole grilled tomatoes from the other plate.

"Excuse me," you say, looking at the two extra places, the two empty chairs, "but are you expecting someone else?"

Aura goes on serving the tomatoes. "No. Señora Consuelo feels a little ill tonight. She won't be joining us."

"Señora Consuelo? Your aunt?"

21

"Yes. She'd like you to go in and see her after supper."

You eat in silence. You drink that heavy wine, occasionally shifting your glance so that Aura won't catch you in the hypnotized stare that you can't control. You'd like to fix the girl's features in your mind. Every time you look away you forget them again, and an irresistible urge forces you to look at her once more. As usual, she has her eyes lowered. While you're searching for the pack of cigarettes in your coat pocket, you touch that big key, and remember, and say to Aura: "Ah! I forgot that one of the drawers in my desk is locked. I've got my papers in it."

And she murmurs: "Then you want to go out?" She says it as a reproach.

You feel confused, and reach out your hand to her with the key dangling from one finger.

"It isn't important. The servant can go for them tomorrow."

But she avoids touching your hand, keeping her own hands on her lap. Finally she looks up, and once again you question your senses, blaming the wine for your bewilderment, for the dizziness brought on by those shining, clear green eyes, and you stand up after Aura does, running your hand over the wooden back of the Gothic chair, without daring to touch her bare shoulder or her motionless head.

You make an effort to control yourself, diverting your attention away from her by listening to the imperceptible movement of a door behind you—it must lead to the kitchen—or by separating the two

22

different elements that make up the room: the compact circle of light around the candelabra, illuminating the table and one carved wall, and the larger circle of darkness surrounding it. Finally you have the courage to go up to her, take her hand, open it, and place your key-ring in her smooth palm as a token.

She closes her hand, looks up at you, and murmurs, "Thank you." Then she rises and walks quickly out of the room.

You sit down in Aura's chair, stretch your legs, and light a cigarette, feeling a pleasure you've never felt before, one that you knew was part of you but that only now you're experiencing fully, setting it free, bringing it out because this time you know it'll be answered and won't be lost . . . And Señora Consuelo is waiting for you, as Aura said. She's waiting for you after supper . . .

You leave the dining room, and with the candelabra in your hand you walk through the parlour and the hallway. The first door you come to is the old lady's. You rap on it with your knuckles, but there isn't any answer. You knock again. Then you push the door open because she's waiting for you. You enter cautiously, murmuring: "Señora . . . Señora . . ."

She doesn't hear you, for she's kneeling in front of that wall of religious objects, with her head resting on her clenched fists. You see her from a distance: she's kneeling there in her coarse woollen nightgown with her head sunk into her narrow shoulders; she's thin, even emaciated, like a medieval sculpture; her

legs are like two sticks, and they're inflamed with
erysipelas. While you're thinking of the continual
rubbing of that rough wool against her skin, she
suddenly raises her fists and strikes feebly at the air,
as if she were doing battle against the images you can
make out as you tiptoe closer: Christ, the Virgin, St.
Sebastian, St. Lucia, the Archangel Michael, and the
grinning demons in an old print, the only happy
figures in that iconography of sorrow and wrath,
happy because they're jabbing their pitchforks into
the flesh of the damned, pouring cauldrons of
boiling water on them, violating the women, getting
drunk, enjoying all the liberties forbidden to the
saints. You approach that central image, which is
surrounded by the tears of Our Lady of Sorrows, the
blood of Our Crucified Lord, the delight of Lucifer,
the anger of the Archangel, the viscera preserved in
bottles of alcohol, the silver heart: Señora Consuelo,
kneeling, threatens them with her fists, stammering
the words you can hear as you move even closer:
"Come, City of God! Gabriel, sound your trumpet!
Ah, how long the world takes to die!"

She beats her breast until she collapses in front of
the images and candles in a spasm of coughing. You
raise her by the elbow, and as you gently help her to
the bed you're surprised at her smallness: she's
almost a little girl, bent over almost double. You
realize that without your assistance she would have
had to get back to bed on her hands and knees. You
help her into that wide bed with its bread crumbs
and old feather pillows, and cover her up, and wait
until her breathing is back to normal, while the

involuntary tears run down her parchment cheeks.

"Excuse me . . . excuse me, Señor Montero. Old ladies have nothing left but . . . the pleasure of devotion . . . Give me my handkerchief, please."

"Señorita Aura told me . . ."

"Yes, of course. I don't want to lose any time. We should . . . we should begin working as soon as possible. Thank you."

"You should try to rest."

"Thank you . . . Here . . ."

The old lady raises her hand to her collar, unbuttons it, and lowers her head to remove the frayed purple ribbon that she hands to you. It's heavy because there's a copper key hanging from it.

"Over in that corner . . . Open that trunk and bring me the papers at the right, on top of the others . . . They're tied with a yellow ribbon."

"I can't see very well . . ."

"Ah, yes . . . it's just that I'm so accustomed to the darkness. To my right . . . Keep going till you come to the trunk. They've walled us in, Señor Montero. They've built up all around us and blocked off the light. They've tried to force me to sell, but I'll die first. This house is full of memories for us. They won't take me out of here till I'm dead! Yes, that's it. Thank you. You can begin reading this part. I will give you the others later. Goodnight, Señor Montero. Thank you. Look, the candelabra has gone out. Light it outside the door, please. No, no, you can keep the key. I trust you."

"Señora, there's a rat's nest in the corner."

"Rats? I never go over there."

"You should bring the cats in here."

"The cats? What cats? Goodnight. I'm going to sleep. I'm very tired."

"Goodnight."

3

That same evening you read those yellow papers written in mustard-coloured ink, some of them with holes where a careless ash had fallen, others heavily fly-specked. General Llorente's French doesn't have the merits his wife attributed to it. You tell yourself you can make considerable improvements in the style, can tighten up his rambling account of past events: his childhood on a hacienda in Oaxaca, his military studies in France, his friendship with the duc de Morny and the intimates of Napoleon III, his return to Mexico on the staff of Maximilian, the imperial ceremonies and gatherings, the battles, the defeat in 1867, his exile in France. Nothing that hasn't been described before. As you undress you think of the old lady's distorted notions, the value she attributes to these memoirs. You smile as you get into bed, thinking of the four thousand pesos.

You sleep soundly until a flood of light wakes you up at six in the morning: that glass roof doesn't have any curtain. You bury your head under the pillow and try to go back to sleep. Ten minutes later you give it up and walk into the bathroom, where you find all your things neatly arranged on a table and your few clothes hanging in the wardrobe. Just as you finish shaving the early morning silence is broken by that painful, desperate yowling.

You try to find out where it's coming from: you open the door to the hallway, but you can't hear anything from there: those cries are coming from up above, from the skylight. You jump up on the chair, from the chair onto the desk, and by supporting yourself on the bookshelf you can reach the skylight. You open one of the windows and pull yourself up to look out at that side garden, that square of yew trees and brambles where five, six, seven cats—you can't count them, can't hold yourself up there for more than a second—are all twined together, all writhing in flames and giving off a dense smoke that reeks of burnt fur. As you get down again you wonder if you really saw it: perhaps you only imagined it from those dreadful cries that continue, grow less, and finally stop.

You put on your shirt, brush off your shoes with a piece of paper, and listen to the sound of a bell that seems to run through the passageways of the house until it arrives at your door. You look out into the hallway. Aura is walking along it with a bell in her hand. She turns her head to look at you and tells you that breakfast is ready. You try to detain her but she goes down the spiral staircase, still ringing that black-painted bell as if she were trying to wake up a whole asylum, a whole boarding school.

You follow her in your shirt-sleeves, but when you reach the downstairs hallway you can't find her. The door of the old lady's bedroom opens behind you and you see a hand that reaches out from behind the partly-opened door, sets a chamberpot in the hallway and disappears again, closing the door.

In the dining room your breakfast is already on the table, but this time only one place has been set. You eat quickly, return to the hallway, and knock at Señora Consuelo's door. Her sharp, weak voice tells you to come in. Nothing has changed: the perpetual shadows, the glow of the votive lights and the silver objects.

"Good morning, Señor Montero. Did you sleep well?"

"Yes. I read till quite late."

The old lady waves her hand as if in a gesture of dismissal. "No, no, no. Don't give me your opinion. Work on those pages and when you've finished I'll give you the others."

"Very well. Señora, would I be able to go into the garden?"

"What garden, Señor Montero?"

"The one that's outside my room."

"This house doesn't have any garden. We lost our garden when they built up all around us."

"I think I could work better outdoors."

"This house has only got that dark patio where you came in. My niece is growing some shade-loving plants there. But that's all."

"It's all right, Señora."

AURA

"I'd like to rest during the day. But come to see me tonight."

"Very well, Señora."

You spend all morning working on the papers, copying out the passages you intend to keep, rewriting the ones you think are especially bad, smoking one cigarette after another and reflecting that you ought to space your work so that the job lasts as long as possible. If you can manage to save at least twelve thousand pesos, you can spend a year on nothing but your own work, which you've postponed and almost forgotten. Your great, inclusive work on the Spanish discoveries and conquests in the New World. A work that sums up all the scattered chronicles, makes them intelligible, and discovers the resemblances among all the undertakings and adventures of Spain's Golden Age, and all the human prototypes and major accomplishments of the Renaissance. You end up by putting aside the General's tedious pages and starting to compile the dates and summaries of your own work. Time passes and you don't look at your watch until you hear the bell again. Then you put on your coat and go down to the dining room.

Aura is already seated. This time Señora Llorente is at the head of the table, wrapped in her shawl and nightgown and coif, hunching over her plate. But the fourth place has also been set. You note it in passing. It doesn't bother you any more. If the price of your future creative liberty is to put up with all the manias of this old woman, you can pay it easily. As you watch her eating her soup you try to figure out her

30

age. There's a time after which it's impossible to detect the passing of the years, and Señora Consuelo crossed that frontier a long time ago. The General hasn't mentioned her in what you've already read of the memoirs. But if the General was forty-two at the time of the French invasion, and died in 1901, forty years later, he must have died at the age of eighty-two. He must have married the Señora after the defeat at Querétaro and his exile. But she would have been only a girl at that time . . .

The dates escape you because now the Señora is talking in that thin, sharp voice of hers, that bird-like chirping. She's talking to Aura and you listen to her as you eat, hearing her long list of complaints, pains, suspected illnesses, more complaints about the cost of medicines, the dampness of the house and so forth. You'd like to break in on this domestic conversation to ask about the servant who went for your things yesterday, the servant you've never even glimpsed and who never waits on table. You're going to ask about him but you're suddenly surprised to realize that up to this moment Aura hasn't said a word and is eating with a sort of mechanical fatalism, as if she were waiting for some outside impulse before picking up her knife and fork, cutting a piece of liver—yes, it's liver again, apparently the favourite dish in this house—and carrying it to her mouth. You glance quickly from the aunt to the niece, but at that moment the Señora becomes motionless, and at the same moment Aura puts her knife on her plate and also becomes motionless, and you remember that the Señora put down her knife only a fraction of a second earlier.

There are several minutes of silence: you finish eating while they sit there rigid as statues, watching you. At last the Señora says, "I'm very tired. I ought not to eat at the table. Come, Aura, help me to my room."

The Señora tries to hold your attention: she looks directly at you so that you'll keep looking at her, although what she's saying is aimed at Aura. You have to make an effort in order to evade that look, which once again is wide, clear, and yellowish, free of the veils and wrinkles that usually obscure it. Then you look at Aura, who is staring fixedly at nothing and silently moving her lips. She gets up with a motion like those you associate with dreaming, takes the arm of the bent old lady, and slowly helps her from the dining room.

Alone now, you help yourself to the coffee that has been there since the beginning of the meal, the cold coffee you sip as you wrinkle your brow and ask yourself if the Señora doesn't have some secret power over her niece: if the girl, your beautiful Aura in her green dress, isn't kept in this dark old house against her will. But it would be so easy for her to escape while the Señora was asleep in her shadowy room. You tell yourself that her hold over the girl must be terrible. And you consider the way out that occurs to your imagination: perhaps Aura is waiting for you to release her from the chains in which the perverse, insane old lady, for some unknown reason, has bound her. You remember Aura as she was a few moments ago, spiritless, hypnotized by her terror, incapable of speaking in front of the tyrant, moving her lips in silence as if she were silently begging you to set her free; so enslaved that she imitated every gesture of the Señora, as if she were permitted to do only what the Señora did.

You rebel against this tyranny. You walk toward the other door, the one at the foot of the staircase, the one next to the old lady's room: that's where Aura must live, because there's no other room in the house. You push the door open and go in. This room is dark also, with whitewashed walls, and the only decoration is an enormous black Christ. At the left there's a door that must lead into the widow's bedroom. You go up to it on tiptoe, put your hands against it, then decide not to open it: you should talk with Aura alone.

And if Aura wants your help she'll come to your room. You go up there for a while, forgetting the yellowed manuscripts and your own notebooks, thinking only about the beauty of your Aura. And the more you think about her, the more you make her yours, not only because of her beauty and your desire, but also because you want to set her free: you've found a moral basis for your desire, and you feel innocent and self-satisfied. When you hear the bell again you don't go down to supper because you can't bear another scene like the one at the middle of the day. Perhaps Aura will realize it, and come up to look for you after supper.

You force yourself to go on working on the papers. When you're bored with them you undress slowly, get into bed, and fall asleep at once, and for the first time in years you dream, dream of only one thing, of a fleshless hand that comes toward you with a bell, screaming that you should go away, everyone should go away; and when that face with its empty eye-sockets comes close to yours, you wake up with a muffled cry, sweating, and feel those gentle hands caressing your face, those lips murmuring in a low voice, consoling you and asking you for affection. You reach out your hands to find that other body, that naked body with a key dangling from its neck, and when you recognize the key you recognize the woman who is lying over you, kissing you, kissing your whole body. You can't see her in the black of the starless night, but you can smell the fragrance of the patio plants in her hair, can feel her smooth, eager body in your arms; you kiss her again and don't ask her to speak.

When you free yourself, exhausted, from her embrace, you hear her first whisper: "You're my husband." You agree. She tells you it's daybreak, then leaves you, saying that she'll wait for you that night in her room. You agree again, and then fall asleep, relieved, unburdened, emptied of desire, still feeling the touch of Aura's body, her trembling, her surrender.

It's hard for you to wake up. There are several knocks on the door, and at last you get out of bed, groaning and still half asleep. Aura, on the other side of the door, tells you not to open it: she says that Señora Consuelo wants to talk with you, is waiting for you in her room.

Ten minutes later you enter the widow's sanctuary.

She's propped up against the pillows, motionless, her eyes hidden by those drooping, wrinkled, dead-white lids; you notice the puffy wrinkles under her eyes, the utter weariness of her skin.

Without opening her eyes she asks you, "Did you bring the key to the trunk?"

"Yes, I think so . . . Yes, here it is."

"You can read the second part. It's in the same place. It's tied with a blue ribbon."

You go over to the trunk, this time with a certain disgust: the rats are swarming around it, peering at you with their glittering eyes from the cracks in the rotted floorboards, galloping toward the holes in the rotted walls. You open the trunk and take out the second batch of papers, then return to the front of the bed. Señora Consuelo is petting her white rabbit. A sort of croaking laugh emerges from her buttoned-up throat, and she asks you, "Do you like animals?"

"No, not especially. Perhaps because I've never had any."

"They're good friends. Good companions. Above all when you're old and lonely."

"Yes, they must be."

"They're always themselves, Señor Montero. They don't have any pretensions."

"What did you say his name is?"

"The rabbit? She's Saga. She's very intelligent. She follows her instincts. She's natural and free."

"I thought it was a male rabbit."

"Oh? Then you still can't tell the difference."

"Well, the important thing is that you don't feel all alone."

"They want us to be alone, Señor Montero, because they tell us that solitude is the only way to achieve saintliness. They forget that in solitude the temptation is even greater."

"I don't understand, Señora."

"Ah, it's better that you don't. Get back to work now, please."

You turn your back on her, walk to the door, leave her room. In the hallway you clench your teeth. Why don't you have courage enough to tell her that you love the girl? Why don't you go back and tell her, once and for all, that you're planning to take Aura away with you when you finish the job? You approach the dooor again and start pushing it open, still uncertain, and through the crack you see Señora Consuelo standing up, erect, transformed, with a military tunic in her arms: a blue tunic with gold buttons, red epaulettes, bright medals with crowned eagles—a tunic the old lady bites ferociously, kisses tenderly, drapes over her shoulders as she performs a few teetering dance steps. You close the door.

"She was fifteen years old when I met her," you read in the second part of the memoirs. "*Elle avait quinze ans lorsue je l'ai connu et, si j'ose le dire, ce sont ses yeux verts qui ont fait ma perdition.*" Consuelo's green eyes, Consuelo who was only fifteen in 1867, when General Llorente married her and took her with him into exile in Paris. "*Ma jeune poupée,*" he wrote in a moment of inspiration, "*ma jeune poupée aux yeux verts; je t'ai comblée d'amour.*" He described the house they lived in, the outings, the dances, the carriages, the world of the Second

36

Empire, but all in a dull enough way. "*J'ai même
supporté ta haine des chats, moi qu'aimais tellement
les jolies bêtes...*" One day he found her torturing a
cat: she had it clasped between her legs, with her
crinoline skirt pulled up, and he didn't know how to
attract her attention because it seemed to him that
"*tu faisais ca d'une façon si innocente, par pur
enfantillage,*" and in fact it excited him so much that
if you can believe what he wrote, he made love to her
that night with extraordinary passion, "*parce que tu
m'avais dit que torturer les chats était ta manière à toi
de rendre notre amour favorable, par un sacrifice
symbolique ...*" You've worked it out: Señora
Consuelo must be a hundred and nine. Her husband
died fifty-nine years ago. "*Tu sais si bien t'habiller,
ma douce Consuelo, toujours drappé dans de velours
verts, verts comme tes yeux. Je pense que tu seras
toujours belle, même dans cent ans ...*" Always
dressed in green. Always beautiful, even after a
hundred years. "*Tu es si fière de ta beauté; que ne
ferais-tu pas pour rester toujours jeune?*"

4

Now you know why Aura is living in this house: to perpetuate the illusion of youth and beauty in that poor, crazed old lady. Aura, kept here like a mirror, like one more icon on that votive wall with its clustered offerings, preserved hearts, imagined saints and demons.

You put the manuscript aside and go downstairs, suspecting there's only one place Aura could be in the morning—the place that greedy old woman has assigned to her.

Yes, you find her in the kitchen, at the moment she's beheading a kid; the vapour that rises from the open throat, the smell of spilt blood, the animal's glazed eyes, all give you nausea. Aura is wearing a ragged, blood-stained dress and her hair is- dishevelled; she looks at you without recognition and goes on with her butchering.

You leave the kitchen: this time you'll really speak to the old lady, really throw her greed and tyranny in

38

her face. When you push open the door she's standing behind the veil of lights, performing a ritual with the empty air, one hand stretched out and clenched, as if holding something up, and the other clasped around an invisible object, striking again and again at the same place. Then she wipes her hands against her breast, sighs, and starts cutting the air again, as if—yes, you can see it clearly—as if she were skinning an animal . . .

You run through the hallway, the parlour, the dining room, to where Aura is slowly skinning the kid, absorbed in her work, heedless of your entrance or your words, looking at you as if you were made of air.

You climb up to your room, go in, and brace yourself against the door as if you were afraid someone would follow you: panting, sweating, victim of your horror, of your certainty. If something or someone should try to enter, you wouldn't be able to resist, you'd move away from the door, you'd let it happen. Frantically you drag the armchair over to that latchless door, push the bed up against it, then fall onto the bed, exhausted, drained of your willpower, with your eyes closed and your arms wrapped around your pillow—the pillow that isn't yours. Nothing is yours.

You fall into a stupor, into the depths of a dream that's your only escape, your only means of saying No to insanity. "She's crazy, she's crazy," you repeat again and again to make yourself sleepy, and you can see her again as she skins the imaginary kid with an imaginary knife. "She's crazy, she's crazy . . ."

in the depths of the dark abyss, in your silent dream with its mouths opening in silence, you see her coming toward you from the blackness of the abyss, you see her crawling toward you.

in silence,

moving her fleshless hand, coming toward you until her face touches yours and you see the old lady's bloody gums, her toothless gums, and you scream and she goes away again, moving her hand, sowing the abyss with the yellow teeth she carries in her blood-stained apron:

your scream is an echo of Aura's, she's standing in front of you in your dream, and she's screaming because someone's hands have ripped her green taffeta skirt in two, and then

she turns her head toward you

with the torn folds of the skirt in her hands, turns toward you and laughs silently, with the old lady's teeth superimposed on her own, while her legs, her naked legs, shatter into bits and fly toward the abyss . . .

There's a knock at the door, then the sound of the bell, the supper bell. Your head aches so much that you can't make out the hands on the clock, but you know it must be late: above your head you can see the night clouds beyond the skylight. You get up painfully, dazed and hungry. You hold the glass pitcher under the tap, wait for the water to run, fill the pitcher, then pour it into the basin. You wash your face, brush your teeth with your worn tooth-brush that's clogged with greenish paste, dampen your hair—you don't notice you're doing all this in

the wrong order—and comb it meticulously in front
of the oval mirror on the walnut wardrobe. Then
you tie your tie, put on your jacket and go down to
the empty dining room, where only one place has
been set—yours.

Beside your plate, under your napkin, there's an
object you start caressing with your fingers: a clumsy
little rag doll, filled with a powder that trickles from
its badly-sewn shoulder; its face is drawn with India
ink, and its body is naked, sketched with a few brush
strokes. You eat the cold supper—liver, tomatoes,
wine—with your right hand while holding the doll in
your left.

You eat mechanically, without noticing at first
your own hypnotized attitude, but later you glimpse
a reason for your oppressive sleep, your nightmare,
and finally identify your sleep-walking movements
with those of Aura and the old lady. You're
suddenly disgusted by that horrible little doll, in
which you begin to suspect a secret illness, a
contagion. You let it fall to the floor. You wipe your
lips with the napkin, look at your watch, and
remember that Aura is waiting for you in her room.

You go cautiously up to Señora Consuelo's door,
but there isn't a sound from within. You look at your
watch again: it's barely nine o'clock. You decide to
feel your way down to that dark, roofed patio you
haven't been in since you came through it, without
seeing anything, on the day you arrived here.

You touch the damp, mossy walls, breathe the
perfumed air, and try to isolate the different
elements you're breathing, to recognise the heavy,

sumptuous aromas that surround you. The flicker of your match lights up the narrow, empty patio, where various plants are growing on each side in the loose, reddish earth. You can make out the tall, leafy forms that cast their shadows on the walls in the light of the match. But it burns down, singeing your fingers, and you have to light another one to finish seeing the flowers, fruits and plants you remember reading about in old chronicles, the forgotten herbs that are growing here so fragrantly and drowsily: the long, broad, downy leaves of the henbane; the twining stems with flowers that are yellow outside, red inside; the pointed, heart-shaped leaves of the nightshade; the ash-coloured down of the grape-mullein with its clustered flowers; the bushy gath-eridge with its white blossoms; the bella-donna. They come to life in the flare of your match, swaying gently with their shadows, while you recall the uses of these herbs that dilate the pupils, alleviate pain, reduce the pangs of childbirth, bring consolation, weaken the will, induce a voluptuous calm.

You're all alone with the perfumes when the third match burns out. You go up to the hallway slowly, listen again at Señora Consuelo's door, then tiptoe on to Aura's. You push it open without knocking and go into the bare room, where a circle of light reveals the bed, the huge Mexican crucifix, and the woman who comes toward you when the door is closed. Aura is dressed in green, in a green taffeta robe from which, as she approaches, her moonpale thighs reveal themselves. The woman, you repeat as she comes close, the woman, not the girl of yesterday:

the girl of yesterday—you touch Aura's fingers, her waist—couldn't have been more than twenty; the woman of today—you caress her loose black hair, her pallid cheeks—seems to be forty. Between yesterday and today, something about her green eyes has turned hard; the red of her lips has strayed beyond their former outlines, as if she wanted to fix them in a happy grimace, a troubled smile; as if, like that plant in the patio, her smile combined the taste of honey and the taste of gall. You don't have time to think of anything more.

"Sit down on the bed, Felipe."

"Yes."

"We're going to play. You don't have to do anything. Let me do everything myself."

Sitting on the bed, you try to make out the source of that diffuse, opaline light that hardly lets you distinguish the objects in the room, and the presence of Aura, from the golden atmosphere that surrounds them. She sees you looking up, trying to find where it comes from. You can tell from her voice that she's kneeling down in front of you.

"The sky is neither high nor low. It's over us and under us at the same time."

She takes off your shoes and socks and caresses your bare feet.

You feel the warm water that bathes the soles of your feet, while she washes them with a heavy cloth, now and then casting furtive glances at that Christ carved from black wood. Then she dries your feet, takes you by the hand, fastens a few violets in her loose hair, and begins to hum a melody, a waltz, to which you dance with her, held by the murmur of her voice, gliding around to the slow, solemn rhythm she's setting, very different from the light movements of her hands, which unbutton your shirt, caress your chest, reach around to your back and grasp it. You also murmur that wordless song, that melody rising naturally from your throat: you glide around together, each time closer to the bed, until you muffle the song with your hungry kisses on Aura's mouth, until you stop the dance with your crushing kisses on her shoulders and breasts.

You're holding the empty robe in your hands. Aura, squatting on the bed, places an object against her closed thighs, caressing it, summoning you with her hand. She caresses that thin wafer, breaks it against her thighs, oblivious of the crumbs that roll down her hips: she offers you half of the wafer and you take it, place it in your mouth at the same time she does, and swallow it with difficulty. Then you fall on Aura's naked body, you fall on her naked arms, which are stretched out from one side of the bed to the other like the arms of the crucifix hanging on the wall, the black Christ with that scarlet silk wrapped around his thighs, his spread knees, his wounded side, his crown of thorns set on a tangled black wig with silver spangles. Aura opens up like an altar.

You murmur her name in her ear. You feel the woman's full arms against your back. You hear her warm voice in your ear: "Will you love me forever?"

"Forever, Aura. I'll love you forever."

"Forever? Do you swear it?"

"I swear it."

"Even though I grow old? Even though I lose my beauty? Even though my hair turns white?'

"Forever, my love, forever."

"Even if I die, Felipe? Will you love me forever, even if I die?"

"Forever, forever. I swear it. Nothing can separate us."

"Come, Felipe, come . . . "

When you wake up, you reach out to touch Aura's shoulder, but you touch only the still-warm pillow and the white sheet that covers you.

You murmur her name.

You open your eyes and see her standing at the foot of the bed, smiling but not looking at you. She walks slowly toward the corner of the room, sits down on the floor, places her arms on the knees that emerge from the darkness you can't peer into, and strokes the wrinkled hand that comes forward from the lessening darkness: she's sitting at the feet of the old lady, of Señora Consuelo, who is seated in an armchair you hadn't noticed earlier: Señora Consuelo smiles at you, nodding her head, smiling at you along with Aura, who moves her head in rhythm with the old lady's: they both smile at you, thanking you. You lie back, without any will, thinking that the old lady has been in the room all the time;

you remember her movements, her voice, her dance, though you keep telling yourself she wasn't there.

The two of them get up at the same moment, Consuelo from the chair, Aura from the floor. Turning their backs on you, they walk slowly toward

the door that leads to the widow's bedroom, enter
that room where the lights are forever trembling in
front of the images, close the door behind them, and
leave you to sleep in Aura's bed.

5

Your sleep is heavy and unsatisfying. In your dreams you had already felt the same vague melancholy, the weight on your diaphragm, the sadness that won't stop oppressing your imagination. Although you're sleeping in Aura's room, you're sleeping all alone, far from the body you believe you've possessed.

When you wake up, you look for another presence in the room, and realize it's not Aura who disturbs you but rather the double presence of something that was engendered during the night. You put your hands on your forehead, trying to calm your disordered senses: that dull melancholy is hinting to you in a low voice, the voice of memory and premonition, that you're seeking your other half, that the sterile conception last night engendered your own double.

And you stop thinking, because there are things even stronger than the imagination: the habits that force you to get up, look for a bathroom off this

room without finding one, go out into the hallway
rubbing your eyelids, climb the stairs tasting the
thick bitterness of your tongue, enter your own
room feeling the rough bristles on your chin, turn on
the bath taps and then slide into the warm water,
letting yourself relax into forgetfulness.

But while you're drying yourself, you remember
the old lady and the girl as they smiled at you before
leaving the room arm in arm; you recall that
whenever they're together they always do the same
things: they embrace, smile, eat, speak, enter, leave,
at the same time, as if one were imitating the other,
as if the existence of one depended on the will of the
other . . . You cut yourself lightly on one cheek as
you think of these things while you shave; you make
an effort to get control of yourself. When you finish
shaving you count the objects in your travelling case,
the bottles and tubes which the servant you've never
seen brought over from your boarding house: you
murmur the names of these objects, touch them,
read the contents and instructions, pronounce the
names of the manufacturers, keeping to these objects
in order to forget that other one, the one without a
name, without a label, without any rational con-
sistency. What is Aura expecting of you? you ask
yourself, closing the travelling case. What does she
want, what does she want?

In answer you hear the dull rhythm of her bell in
the corridor telling you breakfast is ready. You walk
to the door without your shirt on. When you open it
you find Aura there: it must be Aura because you see
the green taffeta she always wears, though her face is

covered with a green veil. You take her by the wrist that slender wrist which trembles at your touch . . .

"Breakfast is ready," she says, in the faintest voice you've ever heard.

"Aura, let's stop pretending."

"Pretending?"

"Tell me if Señora Consuelo keeps you from leaving, from living your own life. Why did she have to be there when you and I . . . Please tell me you'll go with me when . . ."

"Go away? Where?"

"Out of this house. Out into the world, to live together. You shouldn't feel bound to your aunt forever . . . Why all this devotion? Do you love her that much?"

"Love her?"

"Yes. Why do you have to sacrifice yourself this way?"

"Love her? She loves me. She sacrifices herself for me."

"But she's an old woman, almost a corpse. You can't . . ."

"She has more life than I do. Yes, she's old and repulsive . . . Felipe, I don't want to become . . . to be like her . . . another . . ."

"She's trying to bury you alive. You've got to be reborn, Aura."

"You have to die before you can be reborn . . . No, you don't understand. Forget about it, Felipe. Just have faith in me."

"If you'd only explain."

"Just have faith in me. She's going to be out

today for the whole day."

"She?"

"Yes, the other."

"She's going out? But she never . . ."

"Yes, sometimes she does. She makes a great effort and goes out. She's going out today. For all day. You and I could . . ."

"Go away?"

"If you want to."

"Well . . . perhaps not yet. I'm under contract. But as soon as I can finish the work, then . . ."

"Ah, yes. But she's going to be out all day. We could do something."

"What?"

"I'll wait for you this evening in my aunt's bedroom. I'll wait for you as always."

She turns away, ringing her bell like the lepers who use a bell to announce their approach, telling the unwary: "Out of the way, out of the way." You put on your shirt and coat and follow the sound of the bell calling you to the dining room. In the parlour the widow Llorente comes toward you, bent over, leaning on a knobby cane; she's dressed in an old white gown with a stained and tattered gauze veil. She goes by without looking at you, blowing her nose into a handkerchief, blowing her nose and spitting. She murmurs, "I won't be at home today, Señor Montero. I have complete confidence in your work. Please keep at it. My husband's memoirs must be published."

She goes away, stepping across the carpets with her tiny feet, which are like those of an antique doll, and supporting herself with her cane, spitting and sneezing as if she wanted to clear something from her congested lungs. It's only by an effort of the will that you keep yourself from following her with your eyes, despite the curiosity you feel at seeing the yellowed bridal gown she's taken from the bottom of that old trunk in her bedroom.

You scarcely touch the cold coffee that's waiting for you in the dining room. You sit for an hour in the tall, arch-back chair, smoking, waiting for the sounds you never hear, until finally you're sure the old lady has left the house and can't catch you at what you're going to do. For the last hour you've had the key to the trunk clutched in your hand, and now you get up and silently walk through the parlour into the hallway, where you wait for another fifteen minutes—your watch tells you how long—with your ear against Señora Consuelo's door. Then you slowly push it open until you can make out, beyond the spider's web of candles, the empty bed on which her rabbit is gnawing at a carrot: the bed that's always littered with scraps of bread, and that you touch gingerly as if you thought the old lady might be hidden among the rumples of the sheets. You walk over to the corner where the trunk is, stepping on the tail of one of those rats; it squeals, escapes from your foot, and scampers off to warn the others. You fit the copper key into the rusted padlock, remove the padlock, and then raise the lid, hearing the creak of the old, stiff hinges. You take out the third portion of the memoirs—it's tied with a red ribbon—and under it you discover those

51

photographs, those old, brittle dog-eared photographs. You pick them out without looking at them, clutch the whole treasure to your breast, and hurry out of the room without closing the trunk, forgetting the hunger of the rats. You close the door, lean against the wall in the hallway till you catch your breath, then climb the stairs to your room.

Up there you read the new pages, the continuation, the events of an agonized century. In his florid language General Llorente describes the personality of Eugenia de Montijo, pays his respects to Napoleon the Little, summons up his most martial rhetoric to proclaim the Franco-Prussian War, fills whole pages with his sorrow at the defeat, harangues all men of honour about the Republican monster, sees a ray of hope in General Boulanger, sighs for Mexico, believes that in the Dreyfus affairs the honour— always that word "honour"—of the army has asserted itself again.

The brittle pages crumble at your touch: you don't respect them now, you're only looking for a reappearance of the woman with green eyes. "I know why you weep at times, Consuelo. I have not been able to give you children, although you are so radiant with life . . ." And later: "Consuelo, you should not tempt God. We must reconcile ourselves. Is not my affection enough? I know that you love me; I feel it. I am not asking you for resignation, because that would offend you. I am only asking you to see, in the great love which you say you have for me, something sufficient, something that can fill both of us, without the need of turning to sick imaginings . . ." On another page: "I told Consuelo that those medicines were utterly useless. She insists on growing her own herbs in the garden. She says she is not deceiving herself. The herbs are not to strengthen the body, but rather the soul." Later: "I found her in a delirium, embracing the pillow. She cried, 'Yes, yes, yes, I've done it, I've re-created her! I can invoke her, I can give her life with my own life!' It was necessary to call the doctor. He told me he could not quiet her, because the truth was that she was under the effects of narcotics, not of stimulants." And finally: "Early this morning I found her walking barefooted through the hallways. I wanted to stop her. She went by without looking at me, but her words were directed to me. 'Don't stop me,' she said. 'I'm going toward my youth, and my youth is coming toward me. It's coming in, it's in the garden, it's come back . . .' Consuelo, my poor Consuelo! Even the devil was an angel once."

There isn't any more. The memoirs of General Llorente end with that sentence: "*Consuelo, le démon aussi était un ange, avant . . .*"

And after the last page, the portraits. The portrait of an elderly gentleman in a military uniform, an old photograph with these words in one corner: "*Moulin, Photographe, 35 Boulevard Haussmann*" and the date "*1894.*" Then the photograph of Aura, of Aura with her green eyes, her black hair gathered in ringlets, leaning against a Doric column with a painted landscape in the background: the landscape of a Lorelei in the Rhine. Her dress is buttoned up to the collar, there's a handkerchief in her hand, she's wearing a bustle: Aura, and the date "*1876*" in white ink, and on the back of the daguerreotype, in spidery handwriting: "*Fait pour notre dixième anniversaire de mariage*," and a signature in the same hand, "*Consuelo Llorente*". In the third photograph you see both Aura and the old gentleman, but this time they're dressed in outdoor clothes, sitting on a bench in a garden. The photograph has become a little blurred: Aura doesn't look as young as she did in the other picture, but it's she, it's he, it's ... it's you. You stare and stare at the photographs, then hold them up to the skylight. You cover General Llorente's bear with your finger, and imagine him with black hair, and you discover only yourself: blurred, lost, forgotten, but you, you, you.

Your head is spinning, overcome by the rhythms of that distant waltz, by the odour of damp, fragrant plants: you fall exhausted on the bed, touching your cheeks, your eyes, your nose, as if you were afraid that some invisible hand had ripped off the mask you've been wearing for twenty-seven years, the cardboard features that hid your true face, your real appearance, the appearance you once had but then forgot. You bury your face in the pillow, trying to keep the wind of the past from tearing away your own features, because you don't want to lose them. You lie there with your face in the pillow, waiting for what has to come, for what you can't prevent. You don't look at your watch again, that useless object tediously measuring time in accordance with human vanity, those little hands marking out the long hours that were invented to disguise the real passage of

time, which races with a mortal and insolent swiftness no clock could ever measure. A life, a century,
fifty years: you can't imagine those lying measurements any longer, you can't hold that bodiless dust
within your hands.

When you look up from the pillow you find you're
in darkness. Night has fallen.

Night has fallen. Beyond the skylight the swift
black clouds are hiding the moon, which tries to free
itself, to reveal its pale, round, smiling face. It
escapes for only a moment, then the clouds hide it
again. You haven't got any hope left. You don't even
look at your watch. You hurry down the stairs, out
of that prison cell with its old papers and faded
daguerreotypes, and stop at the door of Señora
Consuelo's room, and listen to your own voice,
muted and transformed after all those hours of
silence: "Aura . . ."

Again: "Aura . . ."

You enter the room. The votive lights have gone
out. You remember that the old lady has been away
all day: without her faithful attention the candles
have all burned up. You grope forward in the
darkness to the bed.

And again: "Aura . . ."

You hear a faint rustle of taffeta, and the
breathing that keeps time with your own. You
reach out your hand to touch Aura's green
robe.

"No. Don't touch me. Lie down at my side."

You find the edge of the bed, swing up your legs,
and remain there stretched out and motionless. You

55

can't help feeling a shiver of fear: "She might come back any minute."

"She won't come back."

"Ever?"

"I'm exhausted. She's already exhausted. I've never been able to keep her with me for more than three days."

"Aura . . ."

You want to put your hand on Aura's breasts. She turns her back: you can tell by the difference in her voice.

"No . . . Don't touch me . . ."

"Aura . . . I love you."

"Yes. You love me. You told me yesterday that you'd always love me."

"I'll always love you, always. I need your kisses, your body . . ."

"Kiss my face. Only my face."

You bring your lips close to the head that's lying next to yours. You stroke Aura's long black hair. You grasp that fragile woman by the shoulders, ignoring her sharp complaint. You tear off her taffeta robe, embrace her, feel her small and lost and naked in your arms, despite her moaning resistance, her feeble protests, kissing her face without thinking, without distinguishing, and you're touching her withered breasts when a ray of moonlight shines in and surprises you, shines in through a chink in the wall that the rats have chewed open, an eye that lets in a beam of silvery moonlight. It falls on Aura's eroded face, as brittle and yellowed as the memoirs, as creased with wrinkles as the photographs. You stop kissing those fleshless lips, those toothless gums: the ray of moonlight shows you the naked body of the old lady, of Señora Consuelo, limp, spent, tiny, ancient, trembling because you touch her. You love her, you too have come back . . .

You plunge your face, your open eyes, into Consuelo's silver-white hair, and you'll embrace her again when the clouds cover the moon, when you're both hidden again, when the memory of youth, of youth re-embodied, rules the darkness.

"She'll come back, Felipe. We'll bring her back together. Let me recover my strength and I'll bring her back . . ."

HOW I WROTE

How I Wrote Aura

One, yes, one girl, twenty years of age, in the summer of '61, over twenty-five years ago, crossed the threshold between the small drawing room of an apartment on the Boulevard Raspail and entered the bedroom where I was waiting for her.

There was a rumour of discontent and a smell of explosives in the French capital. These were the years when de Gaulle was finding a way out from Algeria and the OAS, the Secret Army Organization, was indiscriminately blowing up Jean-Paul Sartre and his concierge: the bombs of the generals were egalitarian.

But Paris is a double city; whatever happens there possesses a mirage which seems to reproduce the space of actuality. We soon learn that this is a form of deceit. The abundant mirrors of Parisian interiors do more than simply reproduce a certain space. Gabriel García Márquez says that with their army of mirrors the Parisians create the illusion that their narrow apartments are double the real size. The true mystery—Gabriel and I know this—is that what we see reflected in those mirrors is always *another* time: time past, time yet to be. And that, sometimes, if you are lucky, a person who is *another* person also floats across these quicksilver lakes.

I believe that the mirrors of Paris contain something more than their own illusion. They are, at the same time, the reflection of something less tangible: the light of the city, a light I have attempted to describe many times, in political chronicles of the events of May 1968 and May 1981 and in novels such as *Distant Relations*, where I say that the light of Paris is identical to "the expectation that every afternoon . . . for one miraculous moment, the phenomena of the day—rain or fog, scorching heat or snow—[will] disperse and reveal, as in a Corot landscape, the luminous essence of the Île de France."

A second space: a second person—the other person—in the mirror is not born *in* the mirror: she comes from the light. The girl who wandered in from her living room into her bedroom that hot afternoon in early September more than twenty years ago was another because six years had gone by since I first met her, in the budding grove of her puberty, in Mexico.

But she was also another because the light that afternoon, as if it had been expecting her, defeated a stubborn reef of clouds. That light—I remember it—first stepped through timidly, as if stealing by the menace of a summer's storm; then it transformed itself into a luminous pearl encased in a shell of clouds: finally it spilled over for a few seconds with a plenitude that was also an agony.

In this almost instantaneous succession, the girl I remembered when she was fourteen years old and who was now twenty suffered the same changes as the light coming through the windowpanes: that threshold between the parlour and the bedroom became the lintel between all the ages of this girl: the light that had been struggling against the clouds also fought against her flesh, took it, sketched it, granted her a shadow of years, sculpted a death in her eyes, tore the smile from her lips, waned through her hair with the floating melancholy of madness.

She was another, she had been another, not she who was going to be but she who, always, was being.

The light possessed the girl, the light made love to the girl before I could, and I was only, that afternoon, "a strange guest in the kingdom of love" ("en el reino del amor huésped extraño"), and knew that the eyes of love can also see us with— once more I quote Quevedo—"a beautiful Death."

The next morning I started writing *Aura* in a café near my hotel on the rue de Berri. I remember the day: Khrushchev had just proclaimed his Twenty-Year Plan in Moscow, where he promised communism and the withering away of the state by the eighties—here we are now—burying the West in the process, and his words were reproduced in all their grey minuteness in the *International Herald Tribune*, which was being hawked by ghostly girls, young lovers jailed in brief prisons of passion, the authors of *Aura*: the dead girls.

Two, yes, two years before, I was having a few drinks with Luis Buñuel in his house on the Street of Providence, and we talked about Quevedo, a poet the Spanish film director knew better than most academic specialists on baroque poetry of the seventeenth century.

You have already noticed, of course, that the true author of *Aura* (including the dead girls I have just mentioned) is named Francisco de Quevedo y Villegas, born on September 17, 1580, in Madrid and supposedly deceased on September 8, 1645, in Villanueva de los Infantes: the satirical and scatological brother of Swift, but also the unrivalled poet of our death and love, our Shakespeare, our John Donne, the furious enemy of Góngora, the political agent for the Duke of Osuna, the unfortunate, jailed partisan of fallen power, the obscene, the sublime Quevedo dead in his stoical tower, dreaming, laughing, searching, finding some of the truly immortal lines in the Spanish language:

> Oh condición mortal Oh dura suerte
> Que no puedo querer vivir mañana
> Sin la pensión de procurar mi muerte.

> (Oh mortal state Oh man's unyielding fate
> To live tomorrow I can have no hope
> Without the cost of buying my own death.)

Or maybe these lines, defining love:

Es yelo abrasador, es fuego helado,
es herida que duele y no se siente,
es un soñado bien, un mal presente,
es un breve descanso muy cansado.

(It is freezing fire, a burning ice,
it is a wound that hurts yet is not felt,
a happiness desired, a present evil,
a short but, oh, so tiring rest.)

Yes, the true author of *Aura* is Quevedo, and I am pleased to represent him here today.

This is the great advantage of time: the so-called author ceases to be such; he becomes an invisible agent for him who signed the book, published it, and collected (and goes on collecting) the royalties. But the book was written—it always was, it always is— by others. Quevedo and a girl who was almost dust in love, *polvo enarmorado*. Buñuel and an afternoon in Mexico City, so different from an afternoon in Paris but so different also, in 1959, from the afternoons in Mexico City today.

You could see the two volcanoes, Popocatepetl the smoking mountain and Iztaccihuatl the sleeping lady, as you drove down Insurgentes Avenue, and the big department store had not yet been erected at the corner of Buñuel's house. Buñuel himself, behind a mini-monastery of very high brick walls crowned by crushed glass, had returned to the Mexican cinema with *Nazarín* and was now playing around in his head with an old idea: a filmic transposition of Géricault's painting *Le Radeau de la*

Méduse, which hangs in the Louvre and which describes the drama of the survivors of a naval disaster in the eighteenth century.

The survivors of the good ship *Medusa* at first tried to behave like civilized human beings as they floated around in their raft. But then, as the days went by, followed by weeks, finally by what seemed like an eternity, their imprisonment on the sea cracked the varnish of good manners and they became salt first, then waves, finally sharks: in the end they survived only because they devoured each other. They needed one another to exterminate one another.

Of course, the cinematic translation of the terrible gaze of Medusa is called *The Exterminating Angel*, one of Buñuel's most beautiful films, in which a group of society people who have never truly needed anything find themselves mysteriously incapable of leaving an elegant salon. The threshold of the salon becomes an abyss and necessity becomes extermination: the shipwrecks of Providence Street only need each other to devour each other.

The theme of necessity is profound and persistent in Buñuel, and his films repeatedly reveal the way in which a man and a woman, a child and a madman, a saint and a sinner, a criminal and a dreamer, a solitude and a desire need one another.

Buñuel was inventing his film *The Exterminating Angel* and crossing back and forth, as he did so, over the threshold between the lobby and the bar of his house, looking for all the world like a pensioned picador from old Cagancho's cuadrilla. Buñuel's

66

comings and goings were, somehow, a form of immobility.

> A todas partes que me vuelvo veo
> Las amenazas de la llama ardiente
> Y en cualquier lugar tengo presente
> Tormento esquivo y burlador deseo.

> (Everywhere I turn I see
> The menace of the burning flame
> And everywhere I am aware
> Of aloof torment and mocking desire.)

Since we had been talking about Quevedo and a portrait of the young Buñuel by Dali in the twenties was staring at us, Eluard's poetic formula imposed itself on my spirit that faraway Mexican afternoon of transparent air and the smell of burned tortilla and newly sliced chiles and fugitive flowers: "Poetry shall be reciprocal"; and if Buñuel was thinking of Géricault and Quevedo and the film, I was thinking that the raft of the *Medusa* already contained two eyes of stone that would trap the characters of *The Exterminating Angel* not only in the fiction of a shadow projected on the screen but within the physical and mechanical reality of the camera that would, from then on, be the true prison of the shipwrecks of Providence: a camera (why not?) on top of Lautréamont's poetical meeting of an umbrella and a sewing machine on a dissecting table.

Buñuel stopped midway between lobby and bar and asked aloud: "And if on crossing a doorsill we could instantly recover our youth; if we could be old on *one* side of the door and young as soon as we crossed to the *other* side, what then . . . ?"

Three, yes, three days after that afternoon on the Boulevard Raspail, I went to see a picture that all my friends, but especially Julio Cortázar, were raving about: *Ugetsu Monogatari: The Tales of the Pale Moon After the Rain*, by the Japanese filmmaker Kenji Mizoguchi. I was carrying around with me the first feverish pages of *Aura*, written in that café near the Champs-Elysées as I let my breakfast of coffee and croissants grow cold and forgot the headlines of the morning *Figaro*. "You read the advertisement: this kind of offer is not made every day. You read it and then reread it. It seems addressed to you and to nobody else."

Because "You are Another", such was the subjacent vision of my meetings with Buñuel in Mexico, with the girl imprisoned by the light in Paris, with Quevedo in the freezing fire, the burning ice, the wound that hurts yet is not felt, the happiness desired, the present evil which proclaims itself as Love but was first of all Desire. Curiously, Mizoguchi's film was being shown in the Ursulines Cinema, the same place where, more than thirty years before, Buñuel's *Un Chien Andalou* had first been screened to a vastly scandalized audience. You remember that Red Cross nurses had to be posted in the aisles to help the ladies who fainted when Buñuel, on the screen, slashes the eye of a girl with a razor as a cloud bisects the moon.

The evanescent images of Mizoguchi told the beautiful love story adapted by the Japanese director from the tale "The House among the Reeds", from the collection of the *Ugetsu Monogatari*, written in the eighteenth century by Ueda Akinari, born in 1734 in the red-light district at Sonezaki, the son of a courtesan and an unknown father. His mother abandoned him when he was four years old; he was adopted and raised by a family of paper and oil merchants, the Ueda, with infinite love and care, but also with a profound sense of nostalgia and doom: the happy merchants were unclassed by commerce from their former military tradition; Akinari contracted the pox and was saved perhaps by his adoptive mother's contracting of the disease: she died, he was left crippled in both hands until the God of Foxes, Inari, permitted him to hold a brush and become a calligraphist and, thus, a writer.

But first he inherited a prosperous business; it was destroyed by fire. Then he became a doctor; a little girl whom he was treating died, yet her father continued to have faith in him. So he gave up medicine. He could only be a lame writer, somehow a character in his own stories, persecuted by bad luck, poverty, illness, blindness. Abandoned as a child, Akinari spent his late years dependent on the charity of others, living in temples or the houses of friends. He was an erudite. He did not commit suicide, yet died in 1809.

So with his sick hand miraculously aided by the God of Foxes, Ueda Akinari could take a brush and thus write a series of tales that are unique because they are multiple.

"Originality" is the sickness of a modernity that wishes to see itself as something new, always new, in order continually to witness its own birth. In so doing, modernity is that fashionable illusion which only speaks to death.

This is the subject of one of the great dialogues by the magnificent Italian poet and essayist of the nineteenth century Giacomo Leopardi. Read Leopardi: he is in the wind. I was reading him with joy in the winter of '81, then met Susan Sontag in New York the following spring. She had been surprised by a December dawn in Rome reading Leopardi: like Akinari, infirm; unlike him, a disillusioned romanticist turned pessimistic materialist and maybe, because he knew that in mankind, "outside of vanity, all is pain," he could write some of the most burning lyrical marvels in the Italian language and tell us that life can be unhappy when "hope has disappeared but desire remains intact." For the same reason, he could write the biting dialogue of Fashion and Death:

FASHION: Lady Death! Lady Death!

DEATH: I hope that your hour comes, so that you shall have no further need to call me.

FASHION: My Lady Death!

DEATH: Go to the Devil! I'll come looking for you when you least desire me.

FASHION: But I am your sister, Fashion. Have you forgotten that we are both the daughters of decadence?

Ancient peoples know that there are no words that do not descend from other words and that imagination only resembles power because neither can reign over *Nada*, Nothing, *Niente*. To imagine Nothing, or to believe that you rule over Nothing, is but a form—perhaps the surest one—of becoming mad. No one knew this better than Joseph Conrad in the heart of darkness or William Styron in the bed of shadows: the wages of sin are not death, but isolation.

Akinari's novella is set in 1454 and tells the story of Katsushiro, a young man humiliated by his poverty and his incapacity for work in the fields who abandons his home to make his fortune as a merchant in the city. He leaves his house by the reeds in the care of his young and beautiful wife, Miyagi, promising he will return as the leaves of autumn fall.

Months go by; the husband does not return; the woman resigns herself to "the law of this world: no one should have faith in tomorrow." The civil wars of the fifteenth century under the Ashikaga shoguns make the re-encounter of husband and wife impossible. People worry only about saving their skins, the old hide in the mountains, the young are forcibly drafted by the competing armies; all burn and loot; confusion takes hold of the world and the human heart also becomes ferocious. "Everything," says the author, reminding us that he is speaking from memory, "everything was in ruins during that miserable century."

Katsushiro becomes prosperous and manages to travel to Kyoto. Once settled there, seven years after he bid farewell to Miyagi, he tries to return home but finds that the barriers of political conflict have not fallen, nor has the menace of assault by bandits disappeared. He is fearful of returning to find his home in ruins, as in the myths of the past. A fever takes hold of him. The seven years have gone by as in a dream. The man imagines that the woman, like himself, is a prisoner of time and that, like himself, she has not been able to stretch out her hand and touch the fingers of the loved one.

The proofs of precarious humanity surround Katsushiro; bodies pile up in the streets; he walks among them. Neither he nor the dead are immortal. The first form of death is an answer to time: its name is forgetting, and maybe Katsushiro's wife (he imagines this) has already died; she is but a denizen of the subterranean regions.

So it is death that, finally, leads Katsushiro back to his village: if his wife has died, he will build a small altar for her during the night, taking advantage of the moon of the rainy season.

He returns to his ruined village. The pine that used to identify his house has been struck by lightning. But the house is still there. Katsushiro sees the light from a lamp. Is a stranger now living in his house? Katsushiro crosses the threshold, enters, and hears a very ancient voice say, "Who goes there?" He answers, "It is I, I have come back."

Miyagi recognizes her husband's voice. She comes near to him, dressed in black and covered with grime, her eyes sunken, her knotted hair falling down her back. She is not the woman she had been.

But when she sees her husband, without adding a word, she bursts out crying.

The man and the woman go to bed together and he tells her the reason why he has been so late in returning, and of his resignation; she answers that the world had become full of horror, but that she had waited in vain: "If I had perished from love," she concludes, "hoping to see you again, I would have died of a lovesickness ignored by you."

They sleep embraced, sleep deeply. As day breaks, a vague impression of coldness penetrates the unconsciousness of Katsushiro's dream. A rumour of something floating by awakens him. A cold liquid falls, drop after drop, on his face. His wife is no longer lying next to him. She has become invisible. He will never see her again.

Katsushiro discovers an old servant hidden in a hut in the middle of a field of camphor. The servant tells the hero the truth: Miyagi died many years ago. She was the only woman who never quit the village, in spite of the terrible dangers of war, because she kept alive the promise: we shall see each other once again this autumn. Not only the bandits invaded this place. Ghosts also took up their lodgings here. One day Miyagi joined them.

Mizoguchi's images told a story similar yet different from Akinari's tale. Less innocent, the contemporary filmmaker's story transformed Miyagi into a sort of tainted Penelope, a former courtesan who must prove her fidelity to her husband with greater conviction than a virgin.

When the village is invaded by the troops of

Governor Uesugui sent from Kamakura to fight a ghostly and evasive shogun in the mountains, Miyagi, to save herself from the violence of the soldiers, commits suicide. The soldiers bury her in her garden, and when her husband finally returns, he must appeal to an old witch in order to recover the spectral vision and spectral contact with his dead wife.

Four, no, four years after seeing the film by Mizoguchi and writing *Aura*, I found in an old bookshop in the Trastevere in Rome, where I had been led by the Spanish poets Rafael Alberti and María Teresa Léon, an Italian version of the Japanese tales of the *Togi Boko*, written by Hiosuishi Shoun and published in 1666. My surprise was quite great when I found there, written two hundred years before Akinari's tale and three hundred before Mizoguchi's film, a story called "The Courtesan Miyagino," where this same narrative is told, but this time with an ending that provides direct access to necrophilia.

The returning hero, a Ulysses with no heroism greater than a recovered capacity for forgetting, does not avail himself of a witch to recover his embodied desire, the courtesan Miyagino, who swore to be faithful to him. This time he opens the tomb and finds his wife, dead for many years, as beautiful as the day he last saw her. Miyagino's ghost comes back to tell her bereaved husband this tale.

My curiosity was spurred by this story within the

story of *Aura*, so I went back to Buñuel, who was now preparing the script for his his film *The Milky Way*, reading through the 180 volumes of the Abbé Migne's treatise on patristics and medieval heresies at the National Library in Paris, and asked him to procure me right of entry into that bibliographical sanctuary, more difficult to penetrate, let me add, than the chastity of a fifteenth-century Japanese virgin or the cadaver of a courtesan of the same era and nationality.

Anglo-Saxon libraries, I note in passing, are open to all, and nothing is easier than finding a book on the shelves at Oxford or Harvard, at Princeton or Dartmouth, take it home, caress it, read it, take notes from it and return it. Nothing more difficult, on the contrary, than approaching a Latin library. The presumed reader is also a presumed klepto-maniac, a convicted firebug, and a certified vandal: he who pursues a book in Paris, Rome, Madrid, or Mexico City soon finds out that books are not to be read but to be locked up, become rare and perhaps serve as a feast for rats.

No wonder that Buñuel, in *The Exterminating Angel*, has an adulterous wife ask her lover, a dashing colonel, to meet her secretly in her library. What if the husband arrives? asks the cautious lover. And she answers: We'll tell him I was showing you my incunabula.

No wonder that Juan Goytisolo, when he invades a Spanish library in his *Count Julian*, fruitfully employs his time squashing fat green flies between the pages of Lope de Vega and Axorín.

But let me return to that bibliographical Leavenworth which is the Bibliothèque Nationale in Paris: Buñuel somehow smuggled me in and permitted me to grope in the dark, with fear of imminent discovery, for the ancestry of the Japanese tales of the *Togi Boko*, which in their turn were the forebears of Akinari's tales of the moon after the rain, which then inspired the film by Mizoguchi that I saw in Paris in the early days of September 1961, as I searched for the form and intention of *Aura*.

Is there a fatherless book, an orphan volume in this world? A book that is not the descendant of other books? A single leaf of a book that is not an offshoot of the great genealogical tree of mankind's literary imagination? Is there creation without tradition? But again, can tradition survive without renewal, a new creation, a new greening of the perennial tale?

I then discovered that the ultimate source of this story was the Chinese tale called the "Biography of Ai'King," part of the collection called the *Tsien teng sin hoa*.

Yet, could there conceivably be an "ultimate source" for the story that I saw in a Parisian movie house, thinking I had found in Mizoguchi's dead bride the sister of my Aura, whose mother, I deceived myself, was an image of youth defeated by a very ancient light in an apartment on the Boulevard Raspail and whose father, deceitful as well, was an act of imagination and desire on crossing the threshold between the lobby and the bar of a house in Mexico City's Colonia del Valle?

Could I, could anyone, go beyond the "Biography of Ai'King" to the multiple sources, the myriad, bubbling springs in which this final tale lost itself: the traditions of the oldest Chinese literature, that tide of narrative centuries that hardly begins to murmur the vastness of its constant themes: the supernatural virgin, the fatal woman, the spectral bride, the couple reunited?

I then knew that my answer would have to be negative but that, simultaneously, what had happened did but confirm my original intention: Aura came into this world to increase the secular descent of witches.

Five, at least five, were the witches who consciously mothered Aura during those days of my initial draft in a café near the rue de Berri through which passed, more or less hurried and/or worried by the urgent, immediate events of this world, K.S. Karol the sceptical reporter, Jean Daniel the questioning journalist, and Françoise Giroud the vibrant First Lady of the French press, all of them heading toward the pressroom of *L'Express*, the then great weekly that they had created to fight against bombs and censorship and with the close cooperation—it is hallucinatory to imagine it today—of Sartre and Camus, Mendès-France and Mauriac.

These five bearers of consolation and desire, I believe today, were the greedy Miss Bordereau of Henry James's *Aspern Papers*, who in her turn descends from the cruelly mad Miss Havisham of Charles Dicken's *Great Expectations*, who is herself the English daughter of the ancient countess of Pushkin's *Queen of Spades*, she who jealously keeps the secret of winning at cards.

The similar structure of all three stories only proves that they belong to the same mythical family. You invariably have three figures: the old woman, the young woman, and the young man. In Pushkin, the old woman is the Countess Anna Fedorovna, the young woman her ward Lisaveta Ivanovna, the young man Hermann, an officer of the engineering corps. In Dickens, the old woman is Miss Havisham, the girl Estella, the hero Pip. In Henry James, the old woman is Miss Juliana Bordereau, the younger woman her niece Miss Tina, the intruding young man the nameless narrator H.J.—"Henry James" in Michael Redgrave's staging of the story.

In all three works the intruding young man wishes to know the old lady's secret: the secret of fortune in Pushkin, the secret of love in Dickens, the secret of poetry in James. The young girl is the deceiver—innocent or not—who must wrest the secret from the old woman before she takes it to the grave.

La señora Consuelo, Aura, and Felipe Montero joined this illustrious company, but with a twist: Aura and Consuelo are *one*, and it is *they* who tear the secret of desire from Felipe's breast. The male is now the deceived. This is in itself a twist on machismo.

And do not all three ladies descend from Michelet's medieval sorceress who reserves for herself, be it at the price of death by fire, the secrets of a knowledge forbidden by modern reason, the damned papers, the letters stained by the wax of candles long since gone dead, the cards wasted by the fingers of avarice and fear, but also the secrets of an antiquity projecting itself with greater strength than the future?

For is there a secret more secret, a scandal more ancient, than that of the sinless woman, the woman who does not incite toward sin—Eve—and does not open the box of disgrace—Pandora? The woman who is not what the Father of the Church, Tertullian, would have her be, "a temple built on top of a sewer," not the woman who must save herself by banging a door like Nora in Ibsen's *Doll's House*, but the woman who, before all of them, is the owner of her time because she is the owner of her will and of her body; because she does not admit any division between time, body, and will, and this mortally wounds the man who would like to divide his mind from his flesh in order to resemble, through his mind, his God, and through his flesh, his Devil?

In John Milton's *Paradise Lost*, Adam rebukes the Creator, challenges him, asks him:

> Did I request thee, Maker, from my Clay
> To mould me Man, did I sollicitte thee
> From darkness to promote me, or here place
> In this delicious Garden?

Adam asks his God, and even worse,

> . . . to reduce me to my dust,
> Desirous to resigne, and render back

All I receav'd, unable to performe
The terms too hard, by which I was to hold
The good I sought not.

This man divided between his divine thought and his carnal pain is the author of his own unbearable conflict when he demands, not death, but at least, because she is worse than death, life without Eve— that is, life without Evil, life among men only, a wise creation peopled by exclusively masculine spirits, without this fair defect of nature: woman.

But this life among masculine angels shall be a life alienated, mind and flesh separated. Seen as Eve or Pandora, woman answers from the other shore of this division, saying that she is one, body inseparable from soul, with no complaints against Creation, conceived without sin because the apple of Paradise does not kill: it nurtures and it saves us from the schizoid Eden subverted by the difference between what is to be found in my divine head and what is to be found between my human legs.

The secret woman of James, Dickens, Pushkin, and Michelet who finds her young granddaughter in Aura has, I said, a fifth forebear. Her name is Circe. She is the Goddess of Metamorphosis and for her there are no extremes, no divorces between flesh and mind, because everything is transforming itself constantly, everything is becoming other without losing its anteriority and announcing a promise that does not sacrifice anything of what we are because we have been and we shall be: "Ayer se fue, mañana no ha llegado, / Hoy se está yendo sin parar un

punto; / Soy un fue, y un seré, y un es cansado"
(Yesterday is gone, tomorrow has not come, /
Today is endlessly fleeing; / I am an I was, an I shall
be, an I am tired).

Imitating old Quevedo, I asked the *Aura* papers,
feverishly written as the summer of '61 came to an
end: "Listen, life, will no one answer?" And the
answer came in the night which accompanied the
words written in the midst of the bustle of commerce
and journalism and catering on a grand Parisian
avenue: Felipe Montero, the false protagonist of
Aura, answered me, addressing me familiarly:

You read the advertisement. Only your name is
missing. You think you are Felipe Montero. You
lie to yourself. You are You: You are Another.
You are the Reader. You are what you Read. You
shall be Aura. You were Consuelo.

"I'm Felipe Montero. I read your advertisement."

"Yes, I know . . . Good. Please let me see your
profile . . . No I can't see it well enough. Turn
toward the light. That's right . . ."

You shall move aside so that the light from the
candles and the reflections from the silver and
crystal reveal the silk coif that must cover a head
of very white hair and frame a face so old it must
be almost childlike . . .

"I told you she'd come back."

"Who?"

"Aura. My companion. My niece."

"Good afternoon."

The girl will nod and at the same instant the old lady will imitate her gesture.

"This is Señor Montero. He's going to live with us."

Six, only six days before her death, I met La Traviata. My wife, Sylvia, and I had been invited in September of 1976 to have dinner at the house of our old and dear friends Gabriella and Teddy van Zuylen, who have four daughters with the green eyes of Aura who spy on the guests near four paintings by Roberto Matta, Wifredo Lam, Alberto Gironella, and Pierre Alechinsky, without anyone being able to tell whether the girls are coming in or out of the paintings.

"I have a surprise for you," said our hostess, and she sat me next to Maria Callas.

This woman made me shake violently, for no reason I could immediately discern. While we dined, I tried to speak to her at the same time that I spoke to myself. From the balcony of the Theatre of Fine Arts in Mexico City I had heard her sing *La Traviata* in 1951, when she was Maria Meneghini Callas and appeared as a robust young woman with the freshest, most glorious voice that I had ever heard: Callas sang an aria the same way that Manolete fought a bull: incomparably. She was already a young myth.

I told her so that night in Paris. She interrupted me with a velocity at once velvet-smooth and razor-sharp in its intention: "What do you think of the myth now that you've met her?" she asked me.

"I think she has lost some weight," I dared to answer.

She laughed with a tone different from that of her speaking voice. I imagined that, for Maria Callas, crying and laughing were acts nearer to song than to speech, because I must admit that her everyday voice was that of a girl from the less fashionable neighbourhoods of New York City. Maria Callas had the speaking voice of a girl selling Maria Callas records at Sam Goody's on Sixth Avenue.

This was not the voice of Medea, the voice of Norma, the voice of the Lady of the Camellias. Yes, she had slimmed down, we all knew it, without losing her glorious and warm voice, the voice of the supreme diva. No: no one was a more beautiful woman, a better actress, or a greater singer on an opera stage in the twentieth century.

Callas's seduction, let me add, was not only in the memory of her stage glory: this woman I now saw, thinned down not by her will but by her sickness and her time, nearer every minute to her bone, every second more transparent and tenuously allied to life, possessed a hypnotic secret that revealed itself as *attention*. I really think I have never met a woman who lent more attention to the man she was listening to than Maria Callas.

Her attention was a manner of dialogue. Through her eyes (two black lighthouses in a storm of white petals and moist olives) passed images in suprising mutation: her thoughts changed, the thoughts became images, yes, but only because she was transforming ceaselessly, as if her eyes were the balcony of an unfinished and endless opera that, in everyday life, prolonged in silence the suffused rumour, barely the echo, of the nights which had belonged to Lucia di Lammermoor and Violetta Valéry.

In that instant I discovered the true origin of *Aura*: its anecdotal origin, if you will, but also its origin in desire, since desire is the port of embarkation as well as the final destiny of this novella. I had heard Maria Callas since *La Traviata* in Mexico City when she and I were more or less the same age, twenty years old perhaps, and now we were meeting almost thirty years later and I was looking at a woman I had known before, but she saw in me a man she had just met that evening. She could not compare me to myself. I could: myself and her.

And in this comparison I discovered yet another voice, not the slightly vulgar voice of the highly intelligent woman seated at my right; not the voice of the singer who gave back to bel canto a life torn from the dead embrace of the museum; no, but the voice of old age and madness which, I then remembered (and confirmed it in the Angel record I went out hurriedly to buy the next morning), is the unbelievable, unfathomable, profoundly disturbing voice of Maria Callas in the death scene of *La Traviata*.

Whereas the sopranos who sing Verdi's opera usually search for a supreme pathos achieved thanks to agonizing tremors and an attempt to approach death with sobs, screams, and shudders, Maria Callas does something unusual: she transforms her voice into that of *an old woman* and gives that ancient voice the inflection of madness.

I remember it so well that I can almost imitate the final lines: "E strano! / Cessarono / Gli spasmi del dolore."

But if this be the voice of a hypochondriac old lady complaining of the inconveniences of advanced age, immediately Callas injects a mood of madness into the words of resurgent hope in the midst of a hopeless malady: "In mi rinasce—m'agita / Insolito vigore / Ah! Ma io rittorno a viver'." Only then does death, and nothing but death, defeat old age and madness with the exclamation of youth: "Oh gioia!"

Maria Callas invited Sylvia and me to see her again a few weeks later. But before that, one afternoon, La Traviata died forever. But before, also, she had given me my secret: Aura was born in that instant when Maria Callas identified, in the voice of one woman, youth as well as old age, life along with death, inseparable, convoking one another, the four, finally, youth, old age, life, death, women's names: "*la* juventud," "*la* vejez," "*la* vida," "*la* muerte."

Seven, yes, seven days were needed for divine creation: on the eighth day the human creature was born and her name was desire. After the death of Maria Callas, I reread *The Lady of the Camellias* by Alexandre Dumas *fils*. The novel is far superior to Verdi's opera or to the numerous stage and film adaptations because it contains an element of delirious necrophilia absent from all the descendants.

The novel begins with the return to Paris of Armand Duval—A.D., certainly the double of Alexandre Dumas—who then finds out that Marguerite Gautier had died. Marguerite Gautier, his lover lost through the suspicious will of Duval *père*, who says he is defending the family integrity by demanding that Marguerite abandon Armand, but who is probably envious of his son and would like Marguerite all for himself. Anyway, Duval *fils* hurries desperately to the woman's tomb in Père Lachaise. The scene that follows is surely the most delirious in narrative necrophilia.

Armand obtains permission to exhume the body of Marguerite. The graveyard keeper tells Armand that it will not be difficult to find Marguerite's tomb. As soon as the relatives of the persons buried in the neighbouring graves found out who she was, they protested and said there should be special real estate set apart for women such as she: a whorehouse for the dead. Besides, everyday someone sends her a bouquet of camellias. He is unknown. Armand is jealous of his dead lover: he does not know who sends her the flowers. Ah, if only sin saved us from boredom, in life or in death! This is the first thing that Marguerite told Armand when she met him: "The companion of sick souls is called boredom." Armand is going to save Marguerite from the infinite boredom of being dead.

The gravediggers start working. A pickaxe strikes the crucifix on the coffin. The casket is slowly pulled out; the loose earth falls away. The boards groan frightfully. The gravediggers open the coffin with difficulty. The earth's humidity has made the hinges rusty.

At long last, they manage to raise the lid. They all cover their noses. All, save Armand, fall back.

A white shroud covers the body, revealing some sinuosities. One end of the shroud is eaten up and the dead woman's foot sticks out through a hole. Armand orders that the shroud be ripped apart. One of the gravediggers brusquely uncovers Marguerite's face.

The eyes are no more than two holes. The lips have vanished. The teeth remain white, bare, clenched. The long black tresses, dry, smeared onto the temples, cover up part of the green cavities on the cheeks.

Armand kneels down, takes the bony hand of Marguerite, and kisses it.

Only then does the novel begin: a novel that, inaugurated by death, can only culminate in death. The novel is the act of Armand Duval's desire to find the object of desire: Marguerite's body. But since no desire is innocent—because we not only desire, we also desire to change what we desire once we obtain it—Armand Duval obtains the cadaver of Marguerite Gautier in order to transform it into literature, into *book*, into that second-person singular, the You that structures desire in *Aura*.

You: that word which is mine as it moves, ghostlike, in all the dimensions of space and time, even beyond death.

"You shall plunge your face, your open eyes,

into Consuelo's silver-white hair, and she'll embrace you again when the clouds cover the moon, when you're both hidden again, when the memory of youth, of youth re-embodied, rules the darkness and disappears for some time.

"She'll come back, Felipe. We'll bring her back together. Let me recover my strength and I'll bring her back."

Felipe Montero, of course, is not You. You are *You*. Felipe Montero is only the author of *Terra Nostra*.

Aura was published in Spanish in 1962. The girl I had met as a child in Mexico and seen re-created by the light of Paris in 1961, when she was twenty, died by her own hand, a few years ago, in Mexico, at age forty.